UNPLUGGED Summer

THE SUMMER UNPLUGGED SERIES

CHAPTER 1

It's been twenty four hours. One entire day has passed since my dad picked me up from the county jail, patted me on the back and said, "Son, let's not have this happen again."

The first thing I've noticed about civilian life? Twenty four hours sure pass a hell of a lot faster when you're at home than it does when you're locked in a jail cell. It still feels like I just got out. My chest is tight and my mind keeps falling back to old habits, like expecting to be freezing my ass off at night because I only have one shitty wool blanket. I'm up at the crack of dawn, six a.m. according to my cell phone which is also weird and foreign to me because I went so long without the damn thing.

But I am no longer in jail. I have to keep

reminding myself of this fact. I was arrested, slapped with a four month sentence by a judge who can't stand young guys with promising careers in anything other than bookish college stuff, and I served my time. I'm out. I'm done. I can't keep dwelling on it.

Luckily, county jail wasn't anything like how it's portrayed on TV. There are gangs and the food is shitty and people get their ass beat on a daily basis, but if you stay low and keep to yourself, you'll be okay. At least that's what I was told on my first day by Joshua, the head guard of the C block where I was kept. He was in his mid-twenties and was a huge fan of motocross. He recognized me immediately. I can't even pretend to deny it—he respected me as a local dirt bike racer and therefore he gave me preferential treatment while in jail. I'm grateful for it, that's for damn sure.

I'm lying in my bed, my real bed, at my parent's house in Los Angeles. It's just after six in the morning and I'm wide awake because I'm used to the jail lights being flipped on at six every day. Here, the lights are off and my parents are asleep and the only sound is the gentle hum of the air conditioning.

It is so very refreshing to be back in the real world again.

I make a vow to myself that I won't fuck up to that magnitude ever again.

I don't regret what I did. Luke Brady was asking for an ass whooping, so I gave it to him. I just kind of regret the timing. Had this happened a few months earlier, when I was still seventeen, I probably could have gotten off easier. But now I'm a legal adult, and I get to go to big boy legal adult jail when I screw up.

Never again.

I breathe in deeply, then exhale slowly, counting to ten. I only make it to seven before I'm out of air, so I do it again. It's part of the anger management training they had me take in jail, and while it's relaxing to breathe like this, it doesn't really help me much because I don't have an anger problem. I'm actually a pretty cool guy—at least I think so—and I've never lost my temper in all of my life until that stupid day last winter.

God, what was I thinking?

I'm stuck here in bed, too early to do anything, too alone to distract myself, and these thoughts roll back to me. The day that I screwed it all up. I was at a regional race in Anaheim, at one of the best amateur motocross tracks in the country. We'd all just finished taking a few practice laps before the race would begin and I was feeling good. My bike had new suspension and it ran like a dream. The dirt was perfect and the sun was shining. It was the perfect California day.

I had a girlfriend and I thought things were great.

For the record, this is pretty much exactly where I screwed up. I trusted her. Now I can't even think of her stupid name without thinking of everything she did to screw me over. I call her The Ex in my head now. It gives her less power that way. I even changed her name in my phone to The Ex, and believe me, it's not because I'm still talking to her. It's almost like she had some kind of psychic connection to my jail cell because the moment I got into my dad's truck to drive home yesterday morning, she called me. I didn't get the call until I was back home and charged my phone, but still.

My jaw tightens as I look over at my phone on the nightstand. She's called me five times in the last twenty four hours. I've ignored every one. I'm not sure if I hate her or if I hate myself for trusting her. Maybe it's a little bit of both. The Ex and I have known each other for years. She's a track bunny, the derogatory term for girls who hang out at motocross tracks trying to snag a motocross guy. We'd been friends for a long time and it was never anything more than that because racing is my life and it takes up all of my time. I'd seen her hop from guy to guy (as track bunnies do) but she never dated them very long. She'd always come whining to me, saying guys were stupid.

And I guess she was right about that part because I ended up dating her, which makes me the stupidest one of all.

But when I started dating The Ex a few months before the incident that landed me in jail, I thought it would work out okay. We were friends, so we knew each other's quirks and personalities. It was late one night after a particularly awesome day of racing in which I'd won every moto I entered, and I was high on the win. She'd ambled up to me in her short ass shorts and threw her arms around my neck and said she was so proud of how well I raced that day. Then she kissed me.

I remember thinking it was weird because we were just friends but then there she was, groping me and shoving her tongue in my mouth, and like I said, it was a good day, so I just went with it. Next thing I knew, we were dating.

Things were fine. I liked her, and she liked me. She was always at the track so we saw each other a lot, and she knew everyone there so she didn't whine and complain when I was busy with the races. My other friends always had trouble dating girls who weren't into motocross because they'd get upset when their boyfriend had to go to races every weekend. The Ex was cool with it.

And then the incident happened.

There I was, at the track, on the day of the regional races. Practice was awesome, everything was awesome. Then I rounded the corner and walked by Luke Brady's arrogantly huge motorhome that he drove out to all the races so he could relax in style. And there she was. The Ex. Sucking face with Luke himself, the guy who tried every single weekend to beat me in a race but never could.

"What the fuck?" That's really all I remember saying, even though I've relived this event in my head about a million times over the last four months.

The Ex turned around slowly, untangling herself from Luke's arms, like she wasn't in a hurry. Almost as if she'd planned this. She said something about how I was being a terrible boyfriend who only cared about racing. Luke said something about how he was a better lover than I was and how he was about to be a better racer.

I saw red.

Luke threw the first punch, but I threw the next two dozen. The cops said if I hadn't kept wailing on him after he'd been knocked unconscious, I might not have been punished as severely. I don't know what took over me. Betrayal does that to a guy, I guess. I've been over it in anger management classes multiple times now and it still blows my mind. I am not an angry person. Not usually. Sure, dickhead drivers on the road piss me off, and I'll get upset with myself if I screw up while racing, but I never get that mad. I never assault someone.

But I did, and I have to own it. And now I've paid my debt to society and life goes on while I try to put my own back together. I've often wondered if what The Ex and Luke did to me was done on purpose. Word is, they're still dating, but who knows if that's true because I refuse to get online and check it out.

All I know is that I was barred from racing that day and for the rest of the season due to unacceptable behavior as outlined in the race rules. And

Luke got to race that day without me, which means he won. It was almost as if he planned it.

The guys in jail all say that the best revenge is to live a better life than the ones who wronged you. And that's the problem. I can't figure out how to do that if I'm not back to racing. I've been banned from racing at all the local tracks, and the ban will stay in effect unless my agent can talk them into giving me a second chance.

If that doesn't work out, I'm not sure what the hell I'll do, but my life won't be better in any way, shape, or form, unless I'm on a dirt bike.

CHAPTER 2

By the next day, things haven't changed. It's been forty-eight hours since I became a free man again and I'm still lying in bed, awake early. Yesterday was a complete waste. I'd wanted to go for a run or hit the gym, but all I did was sit around. I even let my mother cook me lunch and dinner like I'm some kind of lazy asshole. She didn't mind and she said I should take a few days to recover from something as traumatizing as jail time.

But now that it's day two, I don't think that's a great idea. I need to get back to my life. I need to sleep later because I used to love sleeping, and then I need to hit the gym and work until my cardio levels are back to where they used to be. I need my dirt bike. I need the track. I need my old life back.

So I force myself to stay in bed another hour, wishing I could fall back asleep. By 7:15, I realize it won't happen, so I climb out of my bed that somehow feels a little too soft now and I put on some track shorts and a pair of running shoes. It's warm enough to go shirtless, and my tan has totally disappeared as of late, so I that's what I do.

I head outside and hit the road and run. Music blasts through my earbuds as I jog, the upbeat rhythm motivating me to run faster and longer than my muscles want me to. There's plenty of weight training in jail, and I did a lot of it, but cardio is harder to come by when you're stuck in a cell the size of a walk in closet. But now I am free. My shoes smack against the pavement while I run, the early summer air is clear in my lungs.

I close my eyes and jog for a while, wishing I could stop but knowing I can't. And then the song stops suddenly, making me open my eyes again. My phone is ringing loudly in my earbuds. I pull it out of my pocket and look at the screen.

The Ex.

Ignoring the call, I start jogging again and I try to get back into the groove of running. I quickly realize that shit won't happen. She has called and she has ruined my morning by making me remember her, and Luke, and the incident. It's as if all of my ambition to get back into shape has just whooshed out of me like a deflated balloon at the end of a kid's birthday party.

I slow to a walk and turn around on the sidewalk, heading back in the direction of home. All I want more than anything is to get back to my old life, the way things used to be before the incident. Before The Ex fucked it all up by being a massive slut.

After I've caught my breath, I call my agent, who answers on the fourth ring. "Adams? You out of the slammer?"

He always calls me by my last name. "Yeah," I say, gazing around at the neighborhood street that's lined with nice homes and palm trees. "I'm out jogging, getting back in shape for my next race."

He snorts. "Ain't happening anytime soon, Adams."

"Why the hell not?" I say without using my anger management techniques.

"You fucked up bad," he says, and I can tell he's a little sorry for me by the tone of his voice. "I mean, I'm trying, don't get me wrong. I get fifteen percent commission from your sponsorships so I care about you man, but you lost all of those when you assaulted a fellow racer."

"I beat up the guy who was sleeping with my girlfriend," I say. "It had nothing to do with motocross."

"Except he was also a motocross racer, Adams. You know this. I'm trying to get you back, okay? Just give me some time."

"Good," I say. I'm moving slower than a freaking snail right now. "Let me know when you hear back from the racing commission."

"I will," he says. "But you might want to start looking at other career choices. You know…just in case."

It takes everything I have not to snap right here and now. Other career choices? There is nothing else for me! I am the fastest racer on the continent and everyone knows it. I'm finally old enough to go pro and all I need is the freaking permission to do it. Motocross is first and foremost about racing dirt bikes, but it's also classified as a family sport so there are conduct rules to follow. The Ex made sure I broke the biggest one.

How the hell is my life ever going to get back to normal now? Either I give up completely and go to college for some bullshit degree for some bullshit job that will never make me happy, or I work harder than I've ever worked. I train and I ride and I prove my worth to the commission. They'll put me back in the races and I'll become the pro racer I've been dreaming I'd be since I was a little kid.

I see our house in the distance and I consider jogging another lap around the block, even though my chest aches and my muscles are exhausted. Maybe this isn't what I'm supposed to do. Maybe I can't just come back home and train like I used to and hope that everything works out. Home is part of the problem. California is where I got arrested. Where I served my time. Where my girlfriend cheated on me, because she made sure to tell me in explicit detail while I was being loaded into the back of a police car that she fucked Luke for weeks before that day when I caught them.

California is where it all went wrong. I need to get away. I've got money saved up from all the years I've been winning races, so theoretically I could go anywhere. But I've only ever lived here in LA. Where the hell else is there to go?

Exotic and beautiful places come to mind. Backpacking through Thailand, jogging on the beach in Maui. But I'm not exactly sure I could bring a bike with me to those places. No, I need somewhere basic. Some place I can train and be alone and get away from all the bullshit of real life here in LA. Preferably a place with no girls fawning over me because their main goal in life is to bang a motocross racer. I need somewhere where no one knows my name. Where I can start fresh and figure out where the hell my life is going to go from here.

And then it hits me.

I don't even remember the name of the town, that's how small and insignificant it is. Five years ago my grandfather died and left everything he had to me because he hated my dad for reasons my dad has never shared with me. He had a house on a few acres and about three thousand dollars in his bank account. It all went into a trust because I was under age at the time but now that I'm eighteen, the property is all mine.

It's a house to live in and land to build a dirt bike track on. And it's in the middle of nowhere. There won't be girls there to distract me, and there won't be camera crews or motocross magazines asking me questions like they would if I went to one of the local dirt bike tracks here. No, it will be perfect.

I can be alone. I can train and get back in shape. I can wait out however long it'll take before

I'm allowed to race again. And the best part is that no girls like The Ex will be there trying to distract me. Girls only lead to trouble, as I've recently discovered. I need to be alone. I need to recharge and start over. This is going to be absolutely perfect.

CHAPTER 3

The flight to Houston is quick, and I have an aisle seat all to myself. I spend the trip looking out the window, trying like hell to forget all the bad things in my life and focus on just the good things, however few of them are left. My parents thought it was weird that I'm choosing to banish myself to the middle-of-nowhere Texas for the summer, but they didn't try to stop me. I have a suitcase of clothes and my dirt bike and gear are being shipped over in a few days. If I can't find some land at this new house to ride, there's a few tracks close by.

I try not to feel like it's a bad omen when I get to the car rental place and the only thing they have available to rent all summer is a shiny red Chevrolet

Malibu. Otherwise known as a soccer mom car. It's about as un-manly of a car as you can get, besides one of those smart things that's the size of a dog crate, and now it's mine for the time being. I spend about two seconds considering buying a truck while I'm here, but I have one at home and it'd be a huge waste of money.

So ugly rental car it is.

I guess I should be thankful that my phone still gets signal all the way out here, otherwise I'd be screwed without my GPS. I'd known Salt Gap, Texas was in the boonies, but as I drive out here, I realize exactly how far out it is. There is nothing but fields and fields of land, farms, gigantic mansions with long driveways and wrought iron fences. My grandfather wasn't a rich man, but the paperwork makes his house look fairly big. There's one thing for sure: Salt Gap has nothing in common with Los Angeles. Like… nothing.

There are no night clubs, no bars, no malls or shopping centers. I don't pass any fancy restaurants, just some hole-in-the-wall diners and cafes that you see on movies and never really expect to see in real life. There is a McDonald's, so at least this town has somewhat been brought into this century. Even though this town is nothing like where I'm from, I feel like I can breathe a little easier here. There won't be any distractions, nothing standing in my way of getting a fresh start. I'll be alone in the house that I now own, and I'll have my dirt bike and that's all that matters.

The GPS shows me my new house and I pull into the driveway. It looks pretty big from here. Two stories, older and kind of Victorian with a big porch. The trust that held this account until I turned eighteen had hired a lawn crew to keep up the landscaping, so the yard looks nice. You can tell the house has been vacant though.

I park and grab my stuff from the back seat, then make my way to the front door. My key works, which is a relief because for a moment I feared it wouldn't. The place smells like an abandoned house, like an old bookstore mixed with pine trees. It's not a horrible smell, but I'll open some windows to air the place out.

It's fully furnished with dusty couches and chairs, and there are old people knick-knacks every-where. I venture around, and check out the place. It's not bad as far as the floorplan goes. Kind of a cool house. All the stuff is super outdated though, but it gives me an idea of what my grandfather was like when he was alive. There's a stuffed deer head above the fireplace, and that kind of gives me the creeps. But the home has a very country feel to it. Kind of like a farm house.

I head to the back door and step onto the back porch. Relief hits me as I look at exactly what I'd hoped I see. Acres of land with nothing in the way of riding my dirt bike. There are only a few trees, and they'll be easy to ride around. No lakes or driveways or anything to get in the way. I can't wait to rent a backhoe and start digging a track. The front yard is also pretty big because all of the houses on this street are set back far from the road and they all have big backyards. My neighbors aren't very close, and there's no home owner's association here like there is back in LA. No one can stop me from digging a track. I'll make a lake in the front of the house and use the dirt to build some jumps in the backyard.

I'm starting to get totally pumped about how great this is. I'm far away from home but no one besides my parents knows where I am. I can ride here instead of going to a track where people will recognize me and want to get autographs or grill me about how I got kicked out of racing. Here, I am invisible.

But first, I'll need some stuff. I make a list of

groceries and toiletries like towels and shampoo. There's probably towels here but I'm not about to use them because by now they're probably more dust than towel. I'll also buy a new TV because the one in here is both tiny and square and so old it should belong in a museum. I plop down on the couch and look around.

This will do.

I can spend my summer here alone with just my thoughts and my dirt bike. I'll get my life back together. When the summer ends and the new season starts, I'll be shape again and faster than ever. My agent will have convinced the board to let me race again.

Yep. Everything will work out just fine.

CHAPTER 4

One week later, I'm all settled in. I feel like some kind of badass adult doing everything all by myself. My dad has always talked about finding independence and becoming a man and all of that, and I think I finally understand what he means. I feel pretty fucking bad ass being out here alone.

Of course, I couldn't do everything alone. Turns out you need a license to operate heavy machinery, but renting the backhoe came with the guy who runs it. He'd never built a dirt bike track before, but we watched some YouTube videos—because everything on earth can be found on there—and we figured it out. There's now a lake in the front yard that's about half filled with water from a recent rain, and now I have five jumps in the back-yard. It's a small track, but it's tight with sharp corners just like the arena cross tracks back home. We roughed up the grass with the blade of the backhoe and made a pathway between the jumps. It's a little rudimentary, but it'll work. And the more I ride on it, the more I can wear the dirt into a real dirt bike track.

The only shitty thing? My bike still isn't here. The shipping company had some problem with heavy rains and construction so my delivery has been delayed. I spend the days watching HBO, which I had installed the day after I got here because really, what kind of a life is it without HBO? And I spend my nights outside near the fire pit, burning some of the firewood my grandfather left piled up near the shed. You can see the stars out here. You can't see anything in LA besides airplanes. It really is beautiful being out here in the middle of nowhere.

It's also lonely.

The Ex still calls me every day, usually a few times. She's resorted to texting now, too, and I've held strong and ignored every single one. I can't lie —sometimes I feel like answering. Sometimes I want to talk to the bitch and ask exactly why she did it. She'd seemed genuinely unremorseful when it all went down, so it doesn't make sense now that she's calling me so much. You don't call someone you cheated on, right?

So yeah, deep down, this stupid part of me wants to talk to her. I just want to know why. But every time I feel like caving and answering her call or responding to her text, I stop myself. I get this vision of Luke Brady sitting next to her, laughing at everything I say. I picture them working together to piss me off more. Every time I do that, it'll piss me off just enough to stop myself from talking to her.

But then it'll be late at night and I'll be sitting by the fire all alone and I wonder if she misses me. If she ever cared about me. If any part of our relationship was even real. When we were together, I was busy all the time. I rode my dirt bike every day, hit the gym every day, raced every weekend. That kind of schedule is hard for girls to handle when they're dating a motocross guy, but The Ex never seemed to mind it because she was already in this world since her little brother was also a racer.

Plus, she left me for Luke, who also rides so that can't possibly be it. I think I was a good boyfriend. I tried, at least. I was loyal and I didn't flirt with other girls. I listened when she talked and I had flowers sent to her house when I didn't get to see her that week. But what do I know? Maybe I suck at everything. Which is why I'm focusing on dirt bikes from now on.

I focus on working out while I wait for my bike to be delivered. I hit the protein shakes before and after my workouts, and I jog a few miles a day to build up cardio. Contrary to what people think, you actually need to be better at cardio than weight training to be fast on a dirt bike. Racing takes a lot out of you, so you have to train hard.

I've taken over one of the guest bedrooms and cleaned out some of the weird stuff that was in here. Now there's just a bed, a nightstand and dresser. I had a new mattress delivered and bought some new sheets for it. The dresser that's here is filled with sheets and linens and I've been too lazy to unpack it and put my stuff in, so I'm living out of a suitcase. But I did make my own personal touches to the room. I brought some posters of Zombie Radio, which is arguably the best rock band on the west coast, and I also brought my good luck poster. It's from when I was thirteen years old and Jeremy Sola gave it to me at the supercross races. I was star struck because Jeremy was a professional racer at the time and I told him I wanted to be just like him. He told me about the importance of training and working hard, and then in addition to signing a poster of himself for me, he grabbed one of the bike model's posters and signed it as well.

The bike models are just hot women who wear skimpy clothing and prance around the dirt bikes at local races. They're on calendars and posters and magazines, always posed next to a bike. My poster has a Yamaha F250 dirt bike on it, with this blonde big boobed model leaning over the front of it. Jeremy signed the poster with these words of advice:

As soon as you look at this poster and see the bike before the girl, you're ready to be a pro racer. -Jeremy Sola

It's kind of dumb I guess, but now I realize more than ever how true it is. I need to focus on the bike. On the sport. Not the girls. Not any girls.

Now that my room feels more like mine, I really enjoy living here. I had thought about taking over the master bedroom but it was just too weird sleeping the room my grandparents used to live in, so yeah. I didn't. My mom has offered to come down and help me clean out the place. We could have a garage sale and get rid of all the junk and then fix up the house to be my vacation home or something. I told her it's a great idea, but I'll have to wait until the summer is over.

This is my summer to be unplugged from everything but motocross.

The next day, I wake up to the ear-splitting wail of a truck backing up. I put on some flip-flops and go outside to where a box truck is slowly reversing down my driveway. It's early as hell and I have to piss, but I rush out anyway because I'm psyched to finally get my bike.

It all arrives in perfect condition. The bike, the gear, and my toolbox. I'm pretty sure the delivery guy thinks I'm some kind of lunatic with how excited I am, but screw him. This is a good day.

I throw on my gear and crank up my bike, reveling in the smell of the exhaust. That's the smell of the greatest sport on earth. I've been dying to check out my makeshift dirt bike track, and now it's finally time.

I rev the throttle, slip on my helmet, and grin as I take off.

CHAPTER 5

Afew days later, I find my grandfather's liquor stash in the pantry. I'm not one for getting wasted or even that drunk, but The Ex has been calling as if she were a bill collector and I owe her a ton of money. She's relentless. She texts me good morning and good night every freaking day even though I'm not responding at all. I'm kind of sick of it all. If she's got so much time to bother me all damn day that means she has to be single. Good. I hope Luke dumped her.

Besides the stupid shit going on with The Ex, my training has come to a grinding halt. I popped a bike tire on a tree root while riding in the backyard today. I'd only had half an hour of practice this morning and then it all went to shit. Plus, the old guy next door came over to bitch at me for riding a bike too early in the morning, so I'm kind of all-around pissed. I pour some whiskey into a glass and take it outside where I build a fire as soon as the sun sets.

Tomorrow, I'll drive two towns over to where there's a motorcycle shop that has a replacement tire for my bike. I checked the town ordinances and since we're so far out in the country and not in city limits, there's not a damn thing the old man next door can do about it. I'll ride my bike whenever I want. Seven in the morning isn't too early, especially on a week day. He can kiss my ass.

Part of me does feel like shit because the last thing I need is to have the neighbors hate me, but I have to train my ass off this summer and they'll have to deal with it.

The fire crackles as I sit here and stare at it, drinking from my whiskey. This is either really chill or really pathetic. I'm not sure which. I should have some friends over or something so it feels like I'm not just some sullen loser sitting around by a fire contemplating all the places in his life where he fucked up.

The whiskey warms my insides and takes off the edge. I've been pissed all day pretty much, and it feels good to relax. Tomorrow I'll get my bike fixed…it'll all be okay. I just need to chill.

When my phone rings, I'm about to lose my shit, but then I see my mom's name on the caller ID. It's a welcome change from seeing The Ex flash across my phone screen.

"Hello?" I say, hoping I don't sound drunk.

"Jacey," she says, which makes me roll my eyes. My name is Jace. Jacey is the ridiculously juvenile baby name she has for me. Only moms can get away with that kind of crap. "How are you doing?"

"I'm good, Mom." I lean back in my chair and stare at the sky. "What's up back at home?"

"Nothing much. Just wanted to check in and see how you're surviving being all alone there."

I laugh. "I'm not alone. I have my dirt bike."

"Honey, I know that girl hurt you but you can't let it make you sulk."

I stiffen. "I'm not sulking, Mom. I'm over that bitch."

"Are you, though?"

I hate how her voice is all soft and sweet like she's afraid she'll hurt my feelings. Since when am I some baby that needs to be handled with kid gloves? "I'm pissed about being kicked out of the races, Mom. That's all. I don't give a shit about that girl anymore. You don't need to worry about me."

She sighs into the phone. "If you say so. I just worry about you."

"You don't need to worry," I say, trying to sound convincing. "My life is all better now. I promise."

When we get off the phone, I'm not sure she believes me. I know she cares about me and all that motherly crap, but it really makes me wonder how pathetic I must look like moving all the way out here after a breakup. Honestly, it's not because of her. It's just not. I'm here for *me*. I am totally over The Ex.

My phone rings a little while later. It's her. I don't know why, but I stand up and put the phone to my ear.

"What?"

There's a long silence, probably because she wasn't expecting me to answer. "Hello to you, too," she says in that voice of hers. The one I've heard so many years of my life, and it never used to sound awful but now it's just the worst. "It's about time you answered my call, Jace."

"You should learn to take a hint," I say, keeping my voice level. She won't get any emotions from me.

She scoffs. "Don't be rude. I just want to talk to you. I've missed you a lot."

It's hard not to laugh out loud. "I don't care what you feel."

"Jace! I said don't be rude! Look, it's been five months, okay? A lot has happened since then and I just want to say hi and tell you I miss you. I really think we could be good together."

I exhale slowly. "You should have thought about that before you fucked that dude."

I don't say his name because he's not worth it.

"Jace! Come on! Stop being stupid! Where are you? Let's go to dinner or something and talk."

I'm feeling pretty damn vindicated that she has no idea I'm not still in California. "Stop calling me," I say. "I don't want to hear from you again, or I swear I'll break this phone in half."

It's a little dramatic, but at this very moment, I believe it. I'll throw the damn thing into the fire. I am so done with this girl and all the bullshit she's put me through. I hang up and don't wait for her answer.

It feels pretty awesome to have told her off, though. Tomorrow will be a better day.

CHAPTER 6

I'm refreshed the next morning. Before I've even poured a bowl of cereal, I feel like a new man already. Maybe telling her off was exactly what I needed, the last piece in the puzzle of starting over my life. The drive to the bike shop takes forever, especially in this slow ass rental car, but eventually I get there and I get my tire and head home as fast as I can. I'm aching to ride my bike again. I feel useless without it.

I usually have a mechanic at the races, someone we hire to take care of my bikes and fix anything that goes wrong so I can focus only on the races. But out here, I'm all alone and I'm happy my dad made me learn how to take care of a bike myself. A lot of these rich ass idiots from Cali only care about riding the bike, not fixing them. But it's a skill you need to know. Not to get all philosophical and shit, but knowing how to take your bike apart and then put it back together again makes you one with the bike. You care more about it when you understand how it works.

I quickly change out the popped tire for the new one and then throw on some riding gear. The stuff I wore yesterday smells like a rank ass locker room, so I grab a clean pair of red and black gear from my suitcase. Motocross gear is kind of like a jersey mixed with protective equipment. The pants have breathable areas so you don't sweat your balls off, but they also have thick patches of leather on the inside so the muffler pipe doesn't burn your legs. My jersey is mostly a mesh fabric to keep you cool and my last name, Adams, is printed on the back of it.

It feels great to be back out here, soaring over jumps and sliding full throttle around the massive sweeper turn I put at the back of the property. I ride all day, only stopping for lunch and to refill with gas, and then I get back on my bike and ride some more.

At dusk, I figure I can ride a few more laps before it's too dark to see. And then my chain busts.

Seriously? What else is going to break on this stupid thing? Maybe I'm riding it too hard. Maybe Fate is just being a huge bitch to me right now.

I pull off my shirt and wipe the sweat from my face, then push my bike back up to the house where there's a porchlight so I can assess the damage. The good news is that I have a new bike chain already, so I won't have to waste time driving to the nearest shop tomorrow.

I pull off the chain and study it, wondering what made it break. Dirt bike chains are thicker and stronger than regular bicycle chains, but they also go through a lot more damage when riding.

A shadow moves in the upstairs balcony of the house next door. I don't bother looking over. It's probably that old guy deciding if he wants to come yell at me again. Then there's a small crashing sound, like glass breaking, and I still don't look up.

The shadow talks. "Oh my God, no!"

It's a female voice, and it sounds like someone younger, not like an old woman. But it also sounded really fake and weird, so I ignore it. Then she talks again. "This sucks!"

She sounds distressed, and I put two and two together. She must have just broken something. I look up, but the shadowy figure has disappeared. A few seconds later, a girl walks out the back door, bending down to where whatever she broke has landed.

I can't help myself, I walk over there.

"Hi," I say, waving so she doesn't get scared out of her mind when she turns and sees some strange dude standing here.

"Hello," she says, standing and facing me. Oddly, she doesn't seem surprised at all to see me here. Most girls freak out when guys appear in the dark. We shake hands. "I'm Bayleigh," she says, her lips twisting into a nervous grin.

My stomach tightens. When I'd heard her cry out, she sounded younger, like a kid. Now I see she's not a kid at all. She's my age. And she's really cute.

But I am not allowed to think that because I've sworn off women and dating and everything that goes with them.

"I'm Jace," I say remembering that we just shook hands. "What happened?"

She cradles some broken glass in her hand. "I dropped it, and it rolled off." She frowns and tosses the pieces down to where the remnants of a snow globe sit on the concrete. "It's definitely not repairable."

"That blows." I take a deep breath and keep the conversation light. "Do you collect snow globes?"

"It was my mom's." She nods toward the room with the balcony. "That room was hers and it still has all of her stuff in it."

"So this is your grandparent's house?" I ask.

She nods. This is good, because there's no way I can spend time thinking about the granddaughter of the guy who hates me. Still, I can't help myself. I have to keep talking. "I don't think I've seen you around here."

"I'm just visiting for the summer. The whole summer." She groans, and I can't say I blame her. This town sucks.

"The whole summer in this hick town?" I say. "Welcome to my nightmare."

She laughs, and then I'm laughing too. She's very adorable when she laughs, but I can't be thinking that right now.

"There's really nothing to do here," she says. "What are your plans for tonight?"

Trying not to think about you, I think. Instead, I shrug and say, "I'm just going to watch HBO."

"I love HBO, but my grandparents don't have cable." She looks so sad, so deprived of such fantastic television. I know I shouldn't, but I can't help myself. I ask if she wants to come over and watch it with me.

"Sure," she says with a shrug. I'm not some kind of girl genius or anything, but it seems like maybe she's excited about it, but she's not letting me know. I know where she's coming from though, because I'm excited she agreed to come over, but I'm not going to show it either.

I take her inside, realizing only a few seconds later that I should have warned her about the state of the place first. "Yeah, umm, I didn't decorate the place," I say, nodding toward a taxidermy quail perched on the mantle. The situation is a little awkward so I duck into the kitchen. "You want a drink? I've got Coke, Mountain Dew, sweet tea…"

Bayleigh smiles. "Coke is cool, thanks." I toss her one and then she says, "So if you didn't decorate the place, who did?"

"My grandfather." As much as I want to sit next to her on the couch, I slide into the recliner instead so I can keep my distance from this girl who gets a little cuter each time I look over at her. She sits on the couch, choosing the seat that's far away from me.

"Do you live with him?" she asks.

"He died a few years ago. Cancer." I gesture

toward the room around us. "Left me the whole house and everything he owned."

She frowns. "I'm sorry for your loss."

"Eh, I never really knew him that well. Him and my dad had a falling out and they never spoke, so I dunno."

"Wow, he left everything to you and you didn't even know him?"

"Well, he had no one else in his life," I say.

"And you just live here without changing anything?" she says, opening her drink.

"Nah, I live in California. I just came here for the summer. Take inventory of what is now mine and all…" I just say some bullshit because I can't let her know the real reason I'm here.

"So you're from the west coast and you like dirt bikes." She smiles, and I've seen that smile before. She's impressed.

"It's a little more than *like*, girl. It's my entire life." I might get a little too emotional here, but I can't help it. Motocross is my entire life, and it's what I'm fighting for.

Her brows pull together. "What do you mean?"

There's no way I can possibly explain it. I'll sound like a lunatic with how obsessed I am, or I'll get angry about Luke or… yeah, I just can't. I change the channel on the TV and pretend like I'm super invested in it. "This movie is hilarious," I say. "Want to watch?"

She nods. "So what do you mean?" she asks again. Now almost want to tell her. But I don't. "Okay fine, don't tell me," she says, turning to the TV.

I am a shit bag. I lean forward. "Sorry, I know that's rude of me, but I'm not in the habit of telling people about my career right now."

"Career?" she says, lifting an eyebrow. "Yeah, you should definitely tell me." She giggles and it makes my stomach hurt because she truly is one of those girls who are just adorable no matter what. She's not even dressed up or covered in makeup, and she's still so fucking cute. "You can't possibly be old enough to have a career," she says.

"I race motocross for a living. You can go pro at eighteen. It's my first year of being pro." I lift my chin a little. "You know, getting paid to ride."

She seems genuinely surprised. "Wow, so you're like really good?"

I nod, but my self-esteem falters because although I'm fast as hell on a bike, the career part of it is kind of hanging in the balance right now.

She must notice the weirdness on my face because she says, "So is it the off season?"

"Not exactly," I say. I turn back to the television because I am so not talking about this anymore. Everyone else I know already thinks I'm a failure in my career. I don't really feel like explaining it to yet another person.

After the movie is over, I offer to give her a grand tour of the house. She says yes, which surprises me in a good way. I'd kind of feared she'd immediately go home. I show her around, pointing out weird things I've noticed in the time I've been here. Like how my grandfather kept every National Geographic magazine for the last twenty years.

When we get to my room, her eyes go wide and she stares at my bed as if she's never seen something so amazing before.

"Jace, I know we don't know each other very well, but do you think I could please, *please* borrow your phone to call my friend real fast?" she says, her knees bending as she pleads with me.

Kind of weird, but whatever. "Sure," I say. "Knock yourself out."

She practically dives toward my phone and begins punching in a number. "Thank you so much. I'll only be a second. It's that my phone…broke…

and I haven't been able to call my best friend for days."

I smile and wave away her excuses. It's really not a big deal. "Yeah, it's cool. I'll just be in the living room when you're done."

"Thanks," she says again. She grins at me and puts the phone to her ear.

I venture back out into the living room, but a few minutes later I hear her gasp as if she's really upset. I can't help myself. I walk back to my room and lean against the door. She spins around when she hears me approach. Anger is etched across her face, my iPhone clenched tightly in her hand.

"Something wrong?" I ask.

She looks me dead in the eyes, and she lies to me. "Nope."

CHAPTER 7

It was hard to sleep last night. It's been hard to sleep a lot of nights lately, but this time the thing keeping me awake wasn't my jail time, The Ex, or my failing motocross career.

It was a girl.

The smart part of my brain is fucking pissed at me for letting one visit with a girl I just met screw me up like this. I know I should be focusing on my bike, my training. Anything but girls. But the stupid part of my brain can't stop thinking about her. It was only one visit, one night, one movie on my couch. I didn't even make a move on her like I would have in the old days back in California. All we did was hang out, and she left rather abruptly after having a phone call.

I'm a little ashamed to admit, but I Googled the phone number she called after she left. Nothing came up, so I guess it was just the cell phone of a friend or something. She'd seemed pretty upset so I can't help wondering if she was talking to a guy. I also can't help but think that if a girl like Bayleigh were *my* girl, I'd never say anything to make her seem so upset on the phone.

But I can't think like that, so I go outside and get ready to ride, only I'm not really feeling it today. I put on my gear and roll my bike out of the shed, then set it on the stand. One of the side panels is a little scuffed up, so I grab a screwdriver and take it off. I don't really know why, because it's not a big deal. I just need something to do with my hands. After it's off, I sit on the porch and stare at the bike, trying to will myself to get on it and ride. For some reason, I'm just not in the mood.

The reason is a girl. And that girl just walked into my backyard. "Hey you," she says.

"Morning," I say, leaning in closer to my bike so I can pretend I'm working on the stupid fender. I have to look at the bike, otherwise I'll see those tight leggings she's wearing and my mind will wander places. Okay, well that didn't work, because it's already wandering to those very places it's not supposed to go.

"I brought you some brownies," she says, holding out a plastic tub.

I grab one and take a bite. The thing is good so I stuff it in my mouth and get back to staring intently at my bike.

"Wow, fatass, you want another one?" she says with this little sarcasm in her tone.

I can't help but smile. I like a girl who can talk shit. "Watch it, girl," I say, taking another brownie from the tub. She laughs and sits next to me, her hand reaching out for the screws from my fender.

"Don't lose those," I tell her. The Ex used to play with stuff when I was working on my bike and she'd always forget where she put it.

"So what are your plans for the day?" Bayleigh asks while she plays with the screws in her palm.

"No one ever has plans in this damn town," I say. "There's nothing you could possibly do here that doesn't involve having a plane ticket to somewhere else." I reach over and take one of the screws from her hand and replace the fender back on the bike.

"I don't have plans either," she says. She stands up and dusts off her ass, which only makes me look at her ass, which is a very bad thing for me. "I brought a stack of DVDs from home, so I'll probably just watch movies all afternoon."

She gives me this little smile and then starts to leave and I know she needs to go and get out of my life and stop tripping me up, but my dumbass starts talking so she won't go. "What kind of movies?"

"About a hundred of them actually." She's grinning sheepishly and I think I love this grin of hers more than the rest of them.

I nod. "I think you should go get that shit immediately," I say. "I'll order us a pizza and we can veg out all night."

Her eyes crinkle at the corners and I can tell I've made her day. She heads home and as much as I want to watch her ass walk away, I slip back inside and brush my teeth real quick, then give my hair a look over in the mirror. Luckily, I haven't been on the bike all day, so I'm not covered in sweat. I look up the number to a pizza place and then call it.

When she gets here, she knocks on the front door, which is kind of adorable. The Ex used to just barge her way into wherever she wanted. My house, my RV, my hotel room. She had no boundaries. I let her inside and pour us each a soda while I tell her about the pizza that'll be here in twenty five minutes. "I also ordered cheese bread but I'm in a pretty horrible mood so I might eat it all."

She doesn't ask why I'm in a horrible mood. I kind of wish she would, although I don't want to talk about it. I guess I just want her to *want* to know about me. Anyhow, we get our food and we watch some movies and I try like hell to stop myself from looking over at her. As much as I know I should stay away from this beautiful girl, the thought of her going home at the end of the night makes me feel lonelier than when I was in jail.

Bayleigh leans forward on the couch. I glance over at her, and she seems like she wants to say something. We've been talking this whole time, but not about anything important. Her lips are flattened, like what she wants to say is very important.

"Do you have a girlfriend back at home?" she says finally.

"Nah," I say, looking at my hands. "Not anymore at least."

"Girlfriends are overrated anyhow," she says with a cute little shrug.

"So you don't have a girlfriend either?" I tease her.

"Oh shut up," she says, but her cheeks redden. She takes another slice of pizza and busies herself by staring at it. "So did you come here by yourself? Why didn't you bring friends or something?"

"I don't have any friends I could spend a summer with," I tell her and I realize it's pretty damn true. My best friend Park is too busy and I don't have anyone else. "They would drive me insane after a week." I want to smile, but now I'm thinking about the reason I'm here and I just can't. "Plus, I deserve to spend a summer alone."

"Why would anyone deserve isolation?" she asks, her eyebrows pulling together in the center. "That's harsh."

"I'm gonna need a drink if I'm going to tell you this story." I stand up and take my empty soda glass into the kitchen. Bayleigh follows me, and when I pour some whiskey into my Coke, she puts her glass next to mine.

"Me too," she says.

I narrow my eyes. "You're too young to drink."

"So are you." She straightens her shoulders.

"So."

She makes this little puppy face. "One shot?"

I sigh, and pour a shot into her soda. I'm not thrilled at being a bad influence on this girl, but I can't say no to those eyes and that little puppy face she just pulled on me. Totally not fair.

Back in the living room, Bayleigh sits next to me, downing her drink faster than she should. I get the feeling she's not like the girls back home who have been drinking themselves into unconsciousness since they were twelve.

I put on another movie and enjoy the closeness of someone so sweet and innocent sitting next to me. There's a pretty good chance she won't steal my wallet and order shit off the internet while I'm not looking. The Ex did that shit. Not this girl.

She sighs and rests her head on my shoulder. My whole body freezes and then floods with a warmth that is not at all what I should be feeling right now. I want to lay my head on top of hers. I want to wrap an arm around her shoulder, or better yet, pull her into my lap. I want to see if those glossy lips of hers taste as good as I'm imagining.

She sighs softly. "This night is exactly what I needed," she whispers.

I reach over and grab her knee and squeeze it gently. "Me too."

CHAPTER 8

This is really fucking bad.

For the last few months, when I wake up all I'm thinking about is my career and how to get it back on track. This morning? I woke up thinking about her. That is not okay. *Why, Jace? Why are you such an idiot?*

Just to take my mind off her, I go for a jog at the crack of dawn. I don't allow myself to look over at her grandparent's house as I jog by; I just stare at the road in front of me and pretend her house doesn't exist. I jog for probably two or three miles before I realize my little escape plan isn't going to work. Jogging doesn't require my mind, just my body. While my legs are moving, my brain is free to think about whatever it wants.

So I turn around and go back home and look around for something to busy my mind instead. I shower quickly because in the shower all I think about is her. Then I get to work unpacking my clothes and organizing my room to make it a little neater and not so disorganized. I load up my iPod with some educational podcasts and then blast the speakers so I can hear it all around the house. Educational podcasts are the perfect thing to think about, right? There are no girls involved in learning about what physicists think causes dark matter.

I find a duster in the laundry room and I go around the whole house, dusting off the years of neglect. I'm not exactly Mr. Chores or anything, so I have to figure out how to do all of this shit. I grab a vacuum and get the floors and then I use the hose attachment thingy to dust off the ceiling fan blades. I'm pretty proud of myself for getting the house clean, but it hasn't taken my mind off of her. She's too pretty to forget about.

Once the house is clean, I dive onto the couch and try to watch some TV, figuring I might be able to find a show interesting enough to take my mind off her. And then I see her DVDs on the TV stand. My heart lights up because I finally have an excuse to see her.

I give myself a once-over in the bathroom mirror, making sure I don't have food in my teeth or anything, and then I grab her DVDs and rush over to her house. Maybe she'll want to hang out and watch more movies with me. Maybe I'll invite her to dinner or something.

My heart pounds as I step up on her porch. This is pretty much enemy territory because I know her grandfather doesn't like me. I stand straight and try to look like a decent human being, and then I ring the doorbell.

What seems like an eternity goes by, but finally I hear the deadbolt click and the door opens. An older woman stands on the other side, one eyebrow cocked like she thinks I'm a door-to-door salesman and she doesn't want any of it.

"Hello," I say, giving her my most charming smile. I hold up the DVDs. "Bayleigh left these at my house yesterday."

"Who are you?" she says, giving me a scrutinizing frown.

"I'm Jace Adams, ma'am. I live next door."

The woman, who I guess is Bayleigh's grandmother, grabs the DVDs from my hand. "She's sick but I'll be sure to give it to her," she says, closing the door.

Well I guess a charming smile can't win her over, especially since her husband kind of totally hates me. I sigh and turn around, then start jogging so I can get out of their yard as soon as possible. I try telling myself that this is a good thing, Bayleigh's grandparents hating me. It means I should just stay away and ignore the girl next door. That fits in perfectly with my plan of ignoring all girls and everything else except dirt bikes.

I should be focusing on dirt bikes.

Not pretty girls with adorable smiles.

CHAPTER 9

I'm not about to go over to Bayleigh's house again, not even if I secretly want to. I call up the guy with the backhoe and he's happy to come back out and help me make a twenty foot long tabletop jump in the backyard. Once it's angled perfectly, I spend the rest of the morning riding around, mostly for fun instead of for speed like usual. I do some whips over the tabletop. They're considered fancy or even "tricks", but really whips aren't hard to do. You throw your bike sideways as you soar over a jump and it looks badass.

I'm doing it hoping Bayleigh might be watching from her upstairs window, but I don't ever look back there to check because I don't want to seem like a show off. Of course, showing off is still showing off even if you act like it isn't. It's probably the lamest thing I've ever done. In my life back home, *every* girl knows who I am. They've seen me race and they know I'm good at what I do. There's no need to impress them with my talent because they already know how good I am.

But Bayleigh was pretty clueless about everything involving motocross and dirt bikes. I think it's really cute how she asked so many questions, and not to mention how refreshing it was to talk to a girl who wasn't already obsessed with me as a racer. My dad always warns about letting the fame get to my head. He says it'll only get worse once I'm a pro racer, and I always roll my eyes and tell him it's not a big deal, but I get what he's saying. It is really easy to become an asshole when girls throw themselves at you. But I don't want to be that type of guy. So it's really nice that Bayleigh is getting to know me, the normal guy, not me, the racer.

Around noon, I take a break from riding and I hang outside by the shed, hoping she'll come out to say hello. I can't even tell if she's seen me or not. The balcony window is shadowed by the overhanging roof so I can't see inside. Not that I'm trying to or anything…

It only takes about ten minutes before I realize I

need to get my shit together and stop stalking this girl. I take a cold shower and head into town to get something to eat. Just about everything that comes with living alone for the summer is great. I can do whatever I want, whenever I want. I can watch anything on TV and keep the AC extra cold without having my mom complain that I'm freezing her out. The only part that sucks is going to a restaurant and eating alone.

I find this burger place that claims to have the best burgers in town, and I order a cheeseburger with jalapenos and a large order of fries and then I tuck into a booth in the corner and read a motocross magazine. I'm not even interested in this stupid thing, but I found it in my car and wanted to look busy and not like I'm some loser who has to eat alone. Most people play on their phones to pretend to look busy, but I have no one to talk to. I could call my mom, but then she'd only go on and on about how much she worries about me and I'm not in the mood for that.

It's a shame Bayleigh broke her phone, or I would have gotten her number the very first day I met her. I could be texting her right now.

Or maybe not, if she's not interested in me.

She did sit really close to me on the couch when

we watched movies. I could feel her body against mine, smell the fruity scent of her shampoo. But she was also drinking, so maybe it didn't mean anything. Guess I won't know until I see her again.

I think Fate is on my side today, because as I'm driving home, I see a girl in shorts and a tank top jogging on the side of the road. She's wearing Converse instead of running shoes, which is a little weird. Her auburn hair sways in a ponytail as she jogs. I slow the car to a crawl and trail along behind her, slowly coming to a stop.

She looks over at me, her eyes wide and a little scared until she sees my car. Her eyes soften. I roll down the window.

"Need a ride?"

For a second, I'm afraid she'll say no and keep running along without me. But then she grins and walks over to the passenger side and slips inside my car. She looks really cute with red cheeks from the sweltering summer heat. I crank the AC for her.

"Thanks," she says, leaning toward the vent and closing her eyes as the cold air washes over her. I'm trying to think of something to say, when she goes, "Nice car," in this sarcastic way.

"It's a rental," I say, tapping the dashboard as if I'm super proud of the thing. I'm hoping to get a smile out of her, and it works. "Yep, this baby was the cheapest model available and she's mine for the whole summer."

She laughs. "You're not going to pick up any girls with a ride this lame."

I lower my voice. "I've already picked up one girl in it." She looks at me, eyes wide, and I wink at her.

And yeah. I can tell it now. She definitely likes me. Maybe not a lot, but I'm winning her over and I couldn't be more excited about it. In this moment, I can't even be bothered to think about my career or all that other stuff I should be thinking about. I just want her to smile at me again.

Too bad we've now reached her house.

"Can you pull in at your house and I'll walk home?" she says, gnawing on her lip.

"Your grandpa doesn't like me, huh?" I pull into my driveway and park under the shade of an old oak tree. "He's never said a word to me, but he's always glaring at me and shit," I tell her, trying to make her feel less guilty than she looks right now.

"He doesn't really like anyone, actually," she says.

I give her a look and she says, "Fine, he doesn't

like you because you're messing up the yard and he thinks it's disrespectful to your dead grandfather."

"Ah…" I look over at her grandparent's house and I realize for the first time that although this place I inherited is all new to me, it holds memories for the man next door. He knew my grandfather and they were friends. I sigh and realize I have been kind of a dick. "Fair enough."

CHAPTER 10

I know I shouldn't be surprised, but apparently when you tell someone to never call you again, that doesn't mean they'll listen to it. In my case, it means they'll keep calling you a few times a day, and when you don't answer, they'll send you a good morning and good night text filled with smiley emojis just to push your buttons.

Really, I don't know why The Ex does this. It's insanely annoying and only makes me hate her more. Does she really think I'll suddenly say, "Well she cheated on me and was a total bitch but she keeps calling and texting so I guess I'll take her back?" She can't possibly think that, yet here she is, texting me again.

I usually allow the anger and hatred of this

woman to rise up in my chest when I see her name on my phone. Usually, I can roll my eyes and think about what a slut she is and then go on with my day. But something is off tonight. My phone keeps lighting up and here I am wishing it was lighting up because of Bayleigh. I wish I wasn't alone here, with no one. I wish I had someone who could be my partner in every sense of the word. Someone who trusted me, who I could trust in return. Someone who wouldn't make the nights be so lonely.

I light a fire in the fire pit as soon as it gets dark. I bought marshmallows the other day thinking it would be fun to roast them, but now that just seems so stupid. Who roasts marshmallows by themselves? That is definitely a friend activity. So I sit in my lawn chair and I watch the fire and I can't stop thinking of her.

I glance up toward her house next door. The back of it is covered in shadows because the back porch light isn't on.

"You out there?" I call out, knowing I won't get a reply.

Only… I hear the creaking of someone stepping onto the balcony. A thin shadowy figure leans out. "Yes," she says. "I just walked out…I wasn't here long or anything."

Thank you, God, for this stroke of good luck.

I wave her over. "Come on down. I could use the company."

The shadow disappears and my heart sinks. But then a few minutes later, I see her tiptoeing from her yard into mine and my whole chest feels fluttery and excited. She sits next to me in the lawn chair I'd set out earlier hoping it would be hers one day.

I nod at her because I'm too nervous to say anything right now. Just being in her presence has got me all tangled up inside. She's so ridiculously beautiful on a normal basis and now the shadows and flickers of the flame give her this romantic, angelic glow.

"This bonfire could use some marshmallows," she says with a little smile.

My phone vibrates so I take it out of my pocket and see The Ex's name on the screen. Although I do have a brand new bag of them in the kitchen, there's no way I could eat right now. "I'll remember that for next time," I say, glancing down at the text.

I've been ignoring all of her hellos and what's ups, but this text is different.

I could be five months pregnant right now and you wouldn't even know, you asshole.

What the hell does that mean? Is it a threat? Is she being serious? Jesus, I can't have a child with that bitch. I can't stand the idea of seeing her ever again. This can't possibly be real.

My thumbs fly across the phone screen, texting her back.

Get Luke and all the other guys you slept with to take a DNA test and tell me the results.

She writes back a few seconds later.

God, Jace. I'm not pregnant. I'm just saying you wouldn't know even if I was because you're being an asshole who won't talk to me in person.

Relief floods over my entire body. Thank God. And then it hits me, like a ton of bricks: she only said that because she knew I'd reply to her. Fuck. I'm not making that mistake again.

I close my fist around my phone and try like hell to look like a normal human being when I glance back at Bayleigh.

"You okay?" she asks sweetly. "You're being super quiet."

I shrug even though I'd rather punch something because I can't believe I was stupid enough to fall for The Ex's shit. "I'm fine. I'm just…I don't know."

She leans forward, her hair falling into her face. "You might as well let it out. It's not like you have anyone else to talk to," she says with a grin. Then she glances at the phone in my hand and says, "Well, anyone who's physically here."

I watch her intently, her soft features glowing in the firelight. I want to ask if she's ever screwed over someone as badly as girls have screwed over me. But I know she hasn't. This girl is sweet. Kind. I put the phone back in my pocket.

"I'm not gonna babble on like some kind of child." I grab a stick from the ground and poke at the logs in the fire. "But, if you have to know, I guess you could just say I've totally ruined my life. I'm stuck. I don't know where to go from here."

"You're eighteen," she says. "Your life isn't over yet. Just like how I know my life isn't technically over, but it sure feels like it."

I lean back in my chair. "What's so bad about your life?"

"Well for starters, I'm stuck here all summer." She glances back toward her house. "Do I even need to go on?"

I snort. "Please do."

She takes a deep breath and lets it out slowly. "I'm stuck here all summer without my friends. I'm grounded from everything, including my phone which is killing me, and my sort of boyfriend just officially became my not-boyfriend."

Okay. I know she's clearly in pain and everything, but damn does it make me happy to hear she doesn't have a boyfriend. I lift an eyebrow. "*Sort of* boyfriend? How is that a thing? Did he ask you to be his *sort of* girlfriend?"

She shakes her head. "Screw you. I don't want to talk about it."

My phone goes off again, but this time it's staying in my pocket. "How did you get grounded?"

She folds her arms across her chest and stares at the fire. "I don't want to talk about that either."

"Okay, I'll go." I pop my knuckles and gather up the courage to spill my guts. Maybe it'll make her want to talk to me as well. "I just lost a two million dollar contract over a fucking girl."

Her mouth falls open, and there's this look in her eyes that I've seen before on other girls. I keep talking. "I had just signed to ride with a factory sponsorship when I lost it all because I got thrown in jail. My agent says there's no way in hell they will give me the contract again now that I'm out.

Apparently motocross is a family sport and they don't think my bad attitude fits in with the family vibe."

"Wait," she says, knitting her brow. "How does a girl play into this?"

I don't want her to know. I don't want to tell her. I want her to keep thinking I'm awesome.

I swallow. "I was in jail for four months on an assault charge." My phone goes off again. I ignore it.

"Did you…" she says, and then she looks away.

I sigh, and take out my phone, clearing away the messages without reading them. The Ex is basically doing the same shit as always, going on and on about how I should talk to her. "He was a guy I raced with, and he pissed me off. He got what he deserved."

"Did you hurt him?" she asks. I can see the fear in her eyes and I hate that I'm the one who caused it. She has nothing to fear from me.

"Oh my God," she says, her eyes widening. "What did you do to him?"

I wave my hand through the air. "He was fine. I just taught him a lesson." I throw my head back and stare at the night sky. I can't help but laugh. "At least I thought I taught him a lesson. He may have fucked my girlfriend but in the end, I'm the one who got fucked."

"I'm sorry," she says. She chews on her bottom lip. This is really awkward for both of us, but I like this girl. I want her to know the truth about me because if she's going to like me back, I want it to be for real. "She never should have done that to you."

"No, she shouldn't. But he knew what he was doing. I was his competition, and he got rid of me." I lift my shoulders then lean back in my chair. "Smart guy."

She doesn't seem super disgusted with me right now, so I guess that's a good thing. "So when you got out of jail you banished yourself to Salt Gap, Texas?"

I nod. "I've officially owned the place ever since I turned eighteen. I never came out to see it because I was too busy. I never understood why a man I'd never met would leave me everything he owned… but maybe he knew I'd need it someday." I grab my iPad off the table next to me and skim through it. "I'm sick of this playlist. I think it's time for some online radio, eh?"

She looks really excited for a moment. "You have WiFi on that thing?"

I nod. "Why are you giving me that look?" I ask.

She leans forward and clasps her hands together in front of her chest, giving me this pleading look. "Do you think…maybe I could…um…?"

And then I remember she got grounded from her stuff, so I roll my eyes and she says, "Could I check my Facebook? Please, just real fast?"

I'm going to let her have it. Hell, she could have anything she wants from me right now because she's just so damn cute, but I like messing with her so I pull the iPad to my chest and give her a look. "Do you think your mother would approve of that?"

"Come on, Jace, pleeease?" She makes this pouty face but all I can think about is how much I love when she says my name. I laugh to try and stop my mind from wandering places it shouldn't go, and then I toss her the iPad.

She gives me this grateful little smile and then she attacks the screen as if logging into her page is the most important thing in the world. I go back to poking at the fire with my stick to give her some privacy. I head back into the kitchen to get us sodas and when I return, she doesn't even seem to notice I'm back. Slowly, I walk up to the back of her chair, and then I lean down and get really close to her.

She doesn't even notice, or if she does, she ignores it.

I hover my lips over her hair, just next to her neck. I want to brush her hair away and kiss her neck, find out of the skin as is soft as it looks. Instead, I exhale. She jumps and squeals and I realize she really didn't know I was standing here. She must have been very absorbed in her Facebook page.

"Dammit Jace, you scared me!" she says, swatting me away.

I laugh. "I've been standing here a while, but you were so damn immersed in writing to your boy toy that you didn't notice."

"He's not my boy toy," she murmurs under her breath.

I fall back into my chair, my heart still pounding from being so close to her. "Whatever you say, Bayleigh. You should forget that dude. You're better than him."

She narrows her eyes. "You should forget that girl, then."

I'm about to tell her exactly how much I hate her, but Bayleigh interrupts me. "You've been texting her all night. So maybe you shouldn't be the one lecturing."

I hold up my hands in surrender. "You're right. I won't text her again. It's not worth it. All we're doing is reminding each other how much we don't get along."

Bayleigh smiles, and this time it's a real smile that makes me all warm inside. "I'm glad you're here," I say, handing her the soda I got from the kitchen. "I came here to take my mind off things but it's hard when I'm all alone."

"Glad I could be of service," she says, winking.

And that wink—it kills me. I want to get up and lift her off the chair and into my arms. I want to carry her inside and throw her on my bed. But I can't do that, not this soon after meeting the girl. I close my eyes and lean back in my chair and tell myself to slow down. If it's meant to be, it will happen on its own time.

But that doesn't mean I can't daydream about her in the meantime.

CHAPTER 11

Maybe I'm being a total gentleman and this is a story that will go down in the history books as the most romantic event in history. Or maybe it'll go down as the stupidest thing a guy has ever done. I take a deep breath and press the doorbell. I guess I'm about to find out.

Bayleigh's grandmother opens the door, a curious expression on her face. "Oh, hello," she says, sounding a little confused.

"Hello," I say, smiling to cover how nervous I am. "Can I speak with your husband for a few minutes, please?"

She looks me up and down, her lips wrinkling into a fine line. "One minute," she says, closing the door. I wait for what feels like a hell of a lot longer than a minute and then when the door opens again, Bayleigh's grandfather appears. He's holding a cup of coffee that smells like he's not a fan of sugar or medium roast.

I stand a little straighter. "Good afternoon, Sir."

He stares at me for a moment, and then closes the door and takes a long sip of his coffee. "What can I do for you?" he asks.

"I'm here to apologize," I say, trying to remember all the things I rehearsed this morning before I came over. Of course now that I'm standing in the presence of this man who loves Bayleigh and hates me, I forget all of it, so I have to make it up as I go along. "I know I arrived very suddenly after a long time of my house being abandoned," I say. "I should have definitely introduced myself first before I brought in a tractor and got to work. I'm Jace Adams, and I'm a professional motocross racer. I came here this summer to get some practice for my career—"

"Aren't there places to do that kind of thing?" he says. "Professional tracks that you can go to?"

"Yes, sir. I just wanted to be alone so I could focus."

He doesn't look like he believes that, but I don't want to go into more details.

"Anyway," I say, clearing my throat. "I understand you and my late grandfather were friends?"

"Yes, Richard and I were very close," he says, his eyebrows wrinkling in the first show of emotion since he stepped out on the porch. "I was sad when he passed away."

"His house is still full of his things." I glance next door. "If you'd like to come over, I'd be happy to let you take any of his stuff that was meaningful to you. I didn't really know him and he has no one else to leave his things to."

"That would be very nice of you," he says with a slight nod.

I can tell I'm starting to win him over and it's the greatest feeling ever. I ask him to tell me about Richard, my late grandfather. He brightens a little —well, as much as a grouchy old man can brighten —and he tells me stories about the man I didn't know. I learn about how they loved fishing together and how my grandfather kept going to church after my grandmother passed away even though he hated it and had only gone to make her happy.

Probably half an hour goes by, and we're still talking. He hasn't explicitly accepted my apology from earlier, but think things are going well. I listen to his stories and I ask questions in an effort to let him see another side of me, the side that's not a selfish asshole punk kid.

"Thank you for coming over," he says after a while. "I'd love to go get Richard's fishing poles later on."

"That'd be great," I say. "Just come over anytime."

"Thank you," he says, offering me a small smile.

Now is my chance. "One more thing," I say. I'm nervous as hell now.

He had been walking back to the door but now he stops and turns to me. "Yes?"

"I noticed the county fair is in town," I say. "I thought it would be fun to invite Bayleigh to go with me. Would that be okay with you?"

He studies me for a long moment, and just when I'm sure he's going to tell me to pound sand, he shrugs. "If she wants to go, she can go."

"Thank you, sir," I say quickly. I don't even try to hide my grin because I know I can't.

"Mhm," he says. "Don't keep her out too late."

The Salt Gap county fair is exactly what I'd expected, which is to say it's not at all like the carnivals back at home. This one has a rodeo and patrol cops on horseback and big jacked up trucks everywhere you look. It's a lot cheaper here in Texas. I pay for Bayleigh and I to get into the fair and she grins the whole time, which makes me wonder if a guy has ever paid for her before.

Bayleigh is cute as hell tonight and it's hard to keep my hands off her. We walk next to each other as we make our way through crowds and vendors and people selling cotton candy and beer. I want to grab her hand but I'm not sure if that would be a welcome gesture right now. We reach the end of a line of booths selling weird country stuff like cowboy boots and big metal signs. This is definitely not like California.

There's a group of teenagers in front of us, all wearing some kind of cowboy attire. Literally every one of them has a cowboy hat and boots, but the girls are kinda slutty with it, pairing their boots with cut off shorts. Bayleigh looks over at me, doing a once over on my jeans and black T-shirt.

"I'm surprised they let us in," she says. "We're not exactly the time of people who come here."

I take her hand under the pretense of guiding her around a group of people who are in our way, but really I just want to feel her palm in mine. "Speak for yourself. I'm wearing my genuine leather chaps under these jeans."

"Really?" she says, eyes widening.

I laugh. "Better watch out. Your gullible is showing."

She rolls her eyes at me but she doesn't let go of my hand. We head toward the carnival games and look for something to play.

"This stuff is totally rigged," she says, lifting an eyebrow when I stop at a booth.

"Yeah, I know," I say, handing some cash to the guy at the ring toss game. "But it's fun."

We play a lot of games and we suck at all of them. At one point, I'm seriously trying to knock over these damn wooden bottles in a triangle and even though I hit them, they don't fall over. Totally rigged. Still, Bayleigh laughs at my attempts, and I feel like getting a laugh out of her is better than winning some stupid game.

Another carnie guy waves me over, promising me that his games are easy enough that I can win something for my *sweetie*. I look over at Bayleigh.

"What do you say…sweetie?" I grin. "Want me to win you something?"

"Only if you let me win you something," she says, snatching the cash from my hand.

Oh man, I like this girl.

The carnie at this booth was right. It's a balloon wall and you get five darts for a dollar. All you have to do is pop a balloon with your dart and you win. I win a cheap stuffed sponge creature that's clearly a knockoff of Spongebob Squarepants.

"Way to go!" the carnie bellows as he hands me the toy.

Bayleigh claps for me. I bow down as I accept her clapping and then present the toy to her. "For you, princess."

"Oooh," she says, batting her eyelashes. "Thank you, noble knight."

With her remaining darts, she pops a yellow balloon. To the carnie, she asks, "What's the most embarrassing thing I can get?"

His bloodshot eyes light up. "I know just the thing!"

I'm assuming it'll be some stupid stuffed animal, but when he turns back around he's holding a plastic necklace. It's a big chain link thing with a massive pendant at the bottom of it. We're talking a pendant the size of a basketball. The carnie wiggles his eyebrows and then presses a switch on the back of it.

It lights up.

The word *bootylicious* blinks across the pendant.

"Oh my God, no," I say.

Bayleigh places the necklace over my head and positions the pendant in the center of my chest. "You look beautiful," she says, giving me this wicked sexy smile. She and the carnie high five. I glare at her, but I'm just playing with her. I have no problem making an ass out of myself it makes her smile.

While we're waiting in line for one of the carnival rides, I can't help but stare at her. My necklace is still glowing in a rainbow of colors, but I refuse to turn it off. Now I think it's embarrassing her more than me. "This is fun," I say. "I never expected my self-inflicted summer punishment would turn out this great."

"Same here. I thought I would have died of boredom by now." She reaches into her back pocket and then frowns, and touches the other one.

"What are you looking for?" I ask.

She looks at her hand, confusion wrinkling her eyebrows. "I don't know," she says, tapping her pockets again. Then she looks up. "Shit. I was looking for my cell phone." She laughs a little, but I can tell it's bothering her. "Ugh, it's such a habit, you know? I can't believe I'm not over it yet."

I put a hand to my chest. "Am I so boring that you need to find someone else to talk to while you're around me?" I shake my head. "Ouch, Bayleigh. I'm heartbroken."

She gives me this look that makes my knees weak. "Maybe I'm having such a great time I felt the need to post it to Facebook or something."

"That's better," I say, smiling.

Hours fly by faster than time should be allowed to go, and soon it's nearly time to leave. I sigh and face the truth. "I promised Ed I'd have you home by eleven," I say, bumping into her shoulder. "That gives us time for one more ride. What will it be?"

"How about something slow?" she says, looking at her empty nacho tray. We've eaten a ton of junk food, so a fast ride wouldn't be a good idea. I look around, then find the Ferris wheel. Perfect.

Something in her demeanor changes as we walk toward it. I slide my arm around her shoulders. "What are you thinking about?"

"Nothing," she says quickly. Her attention is on the Ferris wheel that's currently letting people onto each little carriage. I take my arm off her shoulder just in case it's what's making her uncomfortable.

"Doesn't look like nothing," I say, trying to sound lighthearted. She waits until we've climbed onto the Ferris wheel to answer me.

She shrugs. "I guess I'm just realizing that we had an awesome time tonight, but that only makes the rest of the summer sucky because after tonight, there won't be anything fun to do. At the end of the day, I'm still grounded, I'm still stuck here and I still don't have a phone or computer."

"You can't think that way," I say. I want to touch her, so I run my fingers through a strand of her hair, figuring that's safer than holding her and pulling her close to me like I'd prefer to do. I grin and let my fingers slide through her impossibly soft hair. "Now that Ed doesn't consider me a soulless bastard, I'm sure he'll let you come over. We'll find something fun to do."

Her eyes meet mine. The wheel lurches to a stop at the very top. My stomach tightens. It's not exactly the height that bothers me, but the fact that this thing can be folded up and driven around on an eighteen wheeler when the fair is over. Kind of makes me wonder about the safety of it. She turns to the side and looks over, down at the ground below.

"You're braver than I am," I whisper in her ear.

She turns back toward me, her lips twisted in a little smirk. I can't help myself. I held back long enough and now I can't do it any longer. I kiss her. Slowly, softly, I kiss her. When the ride starts moving again, I reach up and take her head in my hands, holding her steady while we kiss. She leans into me, kissing me back with feeling. It's all the encouragement I need. I wrap my arms around her, part her lips with my tongue. She lets me, and she tastes like candy and soda and everything perfect in this world.

All around us, the world is whooshing by as the Ferris wheel makes one loop after another. I hold onto her, and kiss her like this might be the only chance I get. As the ride starts to slow down, I pull away. Her smile nearly kills me.

I tap a finger on her nose. "You're cute when you're flustered."

CHAPTER 12

The bad thing about Bayleigh's situation is that I can't call her the next morning and tell her how much fun I had on our date last night. I'm sure she knows how I feel, but I hate not being able to tell her. And on top of that, I can't go see her today. I think about leaving a note on her front door, but her grandparents might think I'm a crazy stalker or something, so I leave my house at five in the morning and hope she doesn't feel like I've abandoned her.

I found out last night that my racing agent flew in from California last night to go to a race at a track here in Texas. It's in a town called Mixon, and I've never heard of it at all, but after a quick google search I realized it's becoming a pretty big deal in the motocross world. They're actually having a regionals race there, with plans of hosting a national race next year.

Since my agent promised to get me back in the good graces of the race commission and then promptly stopped answering my calls, I figure there's no better way to talk to him than by finding him in person. Mixon is a few hours away from Salt Gap, but at least it's in the same state. I leave early and I drive straight there.

I pay an entry fee to the girl who looks totally bored to be working there, and then I park and start looking for him. The races are getting ready to start, so there's a ton of people here, and most of them are eagerly waiting for a good day of racing. There's exhaust in the air, and bikes zooming around everywhere. It makes my chest ache to be on my own bike.

Unfortunately, the entire fucking trip is a waste. I don't find him on the first day, so I get a hotel and stay for Sunday's racing. I finally run into the bastard and he tries dodging me, saying he's busy working with some of his Texas clients.

In the end though, I get the answer I'd been dreading. He said he tried his best, but no one wants me racing for them any time soon. I'm considered a hot headed asshole. Someone who isn't a good influence on kids, and most organizations want to sponsor guys who kids can look up to. It's a bunch of bullshit if you ask me.

I can't believe I wasted two days on this shit. The only part that was kind of worthwhile was when I talked with the track's owner. He told me if I ever quit racing, I'd have a job at his place. I could give motocross lessons or something. It all seems kind of weird to me, but I guess he had a point. If my agent is right, everyone kind of hates me, I might not get to race again. But try not to think about that very long because racing is my life.

It's nearly five o'clock when I get back home and all I'm thinking about is her. Well, her and punching a wall. Both sound like great options right now. But I choose her.

I don't even waste any time. The second I pull into my driveway, I cut the engine and jog over to her house.

Her grandmother opens the door and seems surprised to see me here. I hope Bayleigh isn't pissed at me for going MIA for two days. Maybe she told her grandmother about it and now they all hate me.

"Bayleigh!" she calls out, leaving the door open but not exactly inviting me inside.

Bayleigh comes into the room and stops cold when she sees me. "Shit," she says, her cheeks flushing. "Sorry, um—" She's staring at me like she's seen a ghost. "I'll be right back!"

"You'd better," her grandmother calls after her. "Sorry about that," she says to me. "Teenagers…" she shakes her head. I'm not exactly sure why Bayleigh ran away like that, but it probably has something to do with how she was wearing pajamas.

"I've come to ask Bayleigh to dinner," I say in an effort to knock out the uncomfortable silence.

"That would be lovely," she says, giving me a genuine smile. She turns and yells up the stairs, "Your visitor wants to take you to dinner! Please dress appropriately."

A few seconds later, Bayleigh comes running down the stairs, dressed in tight jeans and a black shirt that makes her look knock out gorgeous. The girl must have done this to me on purpose. We say goodbye to her grandmother and then walk out to my car. I open the passenger door for her and she grins up at me as she gets inside.

"So where are we going?" she asks.

"There are literally no good restaurants in town. And I know because I've been to every single one," I say as I buckle my seatbelt. "So I was thinking we'd head out of town and hit up this steakhouse."

"Out of town? Like how far?" she asks while she gazes up at the sunroof. "I'm not sure what my curfew is or anything."

"I've got it taken care of." I reach up to the sunroof and pull back the cover, revealing the evening sky. "There you go."

She smiles and closes her eyes, letting the evening sun shine on her angelic face. I'm glad she's not pissed at me for disappearing the last two days.

"I've had one hell of a time," I say with a sigh. A breeze whips through the car's sunroof and I reach over and brush the hair out of her eyes. "But seeing your pretty face takes all of that away."

She doesn't ask anything about where I've been. And although I didn't want her to get upset with me, it's kind of weird that she doesn't care. A shock of jealousy rises up in my chest. Did she spend the time I was gone talking to that other guy?

I stew over this for a little while. Finally, all I care about is that I'll get to kiss her again. I need to feel her lips on mine, because that's when I truly know what she's thinking. She liked me on the ferris wheel. I hope she still does.

When we reach a red light, I come to a complete stop as fast as I can. "Finally," I say urgently.

"Finally what?" she says.

I lean over and kiss her. All my fears are taken away the moment her lips meet mine. She grabs my arms and holds onto me and kisses me back with all the same passion she had a few days ago. When we pull back, I make fun of her glittery lip gloss just to tease her.

"Sorry," she mumbles.

She is so sweet it's insane. I lean over and place a kiss on her neck. She sighs softly, and it only encourages me to kiss her again, and again, trailing my lips down to her collarbone.

The car behind us honks loudly, startling me and ruining the moment. I look up and the light has turned green.

"Whoops," I say as I step on the gas.

Bayleigh's grin is lopsided, her gaze woozy as we drive off. And now I finally have my answer.

She likes me as much as I like her.

The restaurant seems pretty nice, so I'm hoping it's as good as the online reviews say it is. There's a basket of freshly baked rolls in the middle of our table and I grab one and cover it in butter. Bayleigh watches me.

"So how's your knitting going?" I ask her. I seem to remember her telling me her grandmother was teaching her how to make a blanket.

"You mean crochet?" she says, watching me.

I shrug. "Same thing, right?"

She laughs. "I crocheted a blanket, and it's pretty awesome. But knitting is so not the same thing. I'll let you slide this time, but don't let Grandma hear you talking like that."

"Understood," I say, then I pretend to zip my lips closed. "So where do you normally live? You know, when you aren't banished to your grandparent's house."

"I'm from a small town near Dallas," she says.

My heart leaps. Mixon is near Dallas. "Does it happen to be Mixon?" I ask, hoping like hell that her answer is yes.

Her eyebrows pull together. "Huh? No, I've never heard of that place."

I take another bite of my roll. "Eh, I figured as much. No one lives there."

"What's Mixon?" she asks. "You're from LA, right?"

"Don't worry about it, I'm just…thinking out my options. So," I say, realizing I need to change the subject before I get all pissed off about motocross. "How was your week?"

"Well, I learned how to crochet and I made myself a throw blanket. So, obviously, my week was insanely action-packed and you should be sorry you missed it."

I smile. "I missed you. I wish I could have called or something but…" I point at her and give her a playful grin. "Someone got themselves grounded."

She starts to say something and then she blushes. Luckily for her, our waitress brings our food so the pressure is off her.

"You never answered my question about Mixon," she says after a few minutes.

I gnaw on my bottom lip. "Mixon is a tiny town much like this one, but it's different because Mixon is super famous for its motocross track."

"Oh. So are you going to go ride there or something?"

I shake my head. I can't think about that right now. I can't give up on my dream of going pro. But when I look up, Bayleigh is watching me curiously and I realize I care about her too much to just leave her hanging like that. "I spent the last few days in Mixon. They were hosting a nationals race, and my agent met me there. He was already going to be there and it's just easier to see him at the race than to fly back to LA for a weekend, even though he assured me that either way I saw him would be pointless."

"Why's that?" she asks.

I sigh and run a hand through my hair. As much as I want to run from the truth, I guess it's time to face it. "I guess my career really is over. He claims he did everything he could to get me back in, but no one will allow it. I've been all but excommunicated from professional motocross."

"Excommunicated?" she says, lifting an eyebrow. "That's a thing in motocross?"

I roll my eyes. "Come on, Bayleigh. Your gullible is showing again."

After dinner, I ask her to come back to my house for a little while. She agrees, and I'm happy to spend the time with her. Every second with Bayleigh is a second I'm not stressing about my career. Even though I'll be going back to California after this summer, I can't help but hope that she asks me to stay.

Would I stay?

I can't really answer that question right now. If my career really is as over as my agent says it is, I guess I have no reason to return back home. But every time this thought crosses my mind, my heart rips in half again. This can't possibly be the end of the line for me. There has to be something else.

When we get back to my place, we settle into the couch. Bayleigh lays her head against my shoulder and everything feels right, even if only for a little bit. We flip through channels and try to find something to watch, but really I don't care what's on. I just like being cuddled up next to her.

And then my mom calls. Ugh. "It's my mom," I say, giving her an apologetic look. "I'll be back in a second."

I duck into the other room to take her call. She just wants to chat, as I suspected, but if I hadn't answered then she would have called me back again and again, because that's just how my mom is. I listen to her stories and try to be a good son even though I'm desperately dying to get back to Bayleigh and feel her soft skin in my arms again.

When Mom finally tells me goodnight, I hang up and walk back into the living room. Bayleigh isn't there, so I look around and find her in the kitchen. She's sitting at the table, playing on my iPad. I watch her. She frowns and then types something, waits, and frowns again. Then she replies again. I can tell by the look on her face that she's talking to that guy.

My chest aches. I really thought she was into me, but I guess not. I head back into the living room and sink into the couch, feeling defeated. A few minutes later, she puts down the iPad and looks up at me.

"Why can't you just forget about him?" I ask.

"You don't know who I was talking to," she says defensively. She sits across from me on the loveseat, which totally kills me.

"Then who were you talking to?" I ask. I'm

trying not to sound like some jealous jerk, but I guess I am jealous.

She looks away.

"That's what I thought," I say softly. "You know I was actually *dating* this girl before I came here, she was my real girlfriend, not a *sort of* girlfriend. But I know better than to keep toxic people in my life so I haven't spoken to her since that night at the bonfire. I thought you were on the same page as me, but I guess I was wrong. I guess you prefer guys who treat you like shit."

She stands up abruptly and grabs her purse off the end table. "Shut up, Jace. You aren't allowed to care what I do. You're leaving. You're going back home, and you're leaving and everything we've done together will mean nothing."

She storms to the front door and yanks it open. I follow, but she clearly doesn't want anything to do with me. She levels a glare at me. "So don't even act like I deserve better than Ian, because better guys don't stay around."

CHAPTER 13

I can't stop thinking about what she said. Even now, hours later, when the sun is about to rise on a new day, I'm still pouring over her words in my mind. From the moment I flew here for the summer, I've had every intention of going back home to California. It's where I was born and raised and it's where I want to be. It's the best place for professional motocross, and it's where all my things are.

Bayleigh knows that. And she called me on it last night. She knows I'm leaving and she knows I'm not staying, not here in this shit hole of a town in this run own old person house. It's the truth, after all, even though I don't like admitting it.

Another truth I'm having trouble admitting: I'm falling for the girl next door.

I think about her constantly. I'm dying to see her each day and when she leaves, all I want is to see her again. This is the exact opposite of why I came to Salt Gap for the summer. I'm supposed to be here focusing on my career.

And that's the other thing that keeps me up late at night. My agent has absolutely refused to give me any hope for my career. He's all but told me to fuck off. Actually, he said give it a year or two and he'll try again.

A year or two?

I can't go that long without a job. I can't sit around like some old has-been hoping to get my career back at some arbitrary point in the future. Before I met Bayleigh, this kind of news would have broken me. I'd probably have fallen off the deep end, dove into alcohol and slutty girls in an attempt to drown my pain. So maybe meeting her was on purpose, some divine part of life's plan to make sure I'd land on two feet after my racing career spiraled out of control.

Maybe Bayleigh is my future.

And she's pissed at me right now, so great job Jace.

I spend all day cleaning up the house and organizing my late grandparent's stuff into piles to donate to the Goodwill. I'll ask Bayleigh's grandfather to take one last look through everything before I donate it, and then I can start moving my own stuff in. I don't know how long I'd stay here, because there's not much to do in Salt Gap, but the house is still mine, after all, so I should make it mine.

I set my GPS to the local Home Depot and it's over an hour away, which shouldn't surprise me as much as it does. I go through the aisles with my shopping cart, getting items I desperately need for the house. Cleaning products, new weather-stripping for the back door, a new ceiling fan for my bedroom. I get a few cans of paint to make the inside look nicer and then I talk to a guy in the bathroom department about maybe updating the bathrooms. If I'm going to stay here longer than the summer, I should fix up the house and make it easier to live in.

I can't believe I'm even thinking this. Of staying here in Texas… but it's the only thing I'm thinking right now.

The nearest Home Depot was an hour away from my house, so on the drive home, I decide to take a huge leap into the great unknown. It might not work out, and even if it does, Bayleigh might still hate me. But I have to try.

Jim Fisher picks up on the second ring. "Hello?"

With one hand on the wheel, I grip the phone to my ear. "Hi, Mr. Fisher. This is Jace Adams."

"Wow, Jace? How are you?" Even on the phone, he seems just as star-struck as he was when I met him at his motocross track last weekend.

"I'm doing okay." I take a deep breath and tell myself I'm doing this for her. If I find a way to stay in Texas, then, maybe she'll want to be with me. "I've been thinking a lot about what we talked about the other day."

"Which part?" he asks. My heart races. Was he only joking about offering me a job?

"Well, you mentioned maybe hiring me to work with you," I say, suddenly losing all my confidence.

"That would be amazing," Mr. Fisher says excitedly. "Are you seriously considering it?"

Boom, just like that, my confidence is back. "Yes, sir. My agent doesn't think I'll be racing any time soon and I'd like to stay in the motocross world if I need to get a real job."

He laughs. "Son, I'd love to have you aboard. I

know I'd have clients lined up down the block to get a lesson with you."

"Even with my criminal record?" I ask.

He chuckles. "No one cares about that, Jace. I promise you. If you'd like the job, come on down and we'll figure it out."

I'm smiling so big it makes my cheeks hurt. "Thank you, sir. I'll be seeing you soon."

I tap my fingers on the steering wheel while I drive. I have a job. I have a job! I'm going to stay in Texas! Holy shit, this is happening. Now all I have to do is win over the girl of my dreams. Judging by the way she looked at me last night, that might be harder than trying to get back into professional motocross.

The sun has just set by the time I make it back to Salt Gap. My car's trunk and backseat are filled with home improvement stuff and I'm wearing old jeans and an older T-shirt. This isn't really the best time for a grand romantic gesture.

Which is what makes it a great time. I pull over at the gas station closest to my house and go inside. There was something I saw here last time, and I'm glad I remembered it. In the back, near the cases of beer and cell phone chargers, is a little basket of fresh roses.

To my annoyance, there's only one left in the basket, but it's a beautiful long stem pink rose and it'll have to do. The nearest florist is probably two hours away and it'd be closed by now. I buy the rose and the cashier winks at me as if we're sharing some kind of secret.

"Thanks, man," I say as I take the rose and head back to my car. The only secret here is that I'm in love with Bayleigh and I need to make her mine.

CHAPTER 14

I'm thinking of exactly what I'll say to Bayleigh's grandparents when they open the door. If it's her grandmother, she'll probably be lenient and let me see Bayleigh for a little while. If it's Ed, I might be screwed, but I'll ask to talk to her on the porch.

As I drive past her house, I notice that Ed's Ford truck isn't in the driveway, but another car I've never seen is there. That's odd. Hopefully she's still home. I pull into my driveway and cut the engine. That's when I see it.

Her porch light is on, and Bayleigh's standing there on the porch, facing someone who sits on the porch swing. Her arms are on her hips and she's standing like she's kind of hostile. I get out of my car and walk over to the passenger seat where I've set the rose to make sure it didn't get messed up. I close the door and look over at her house, wondering if I should wait until her visitor is gone before I go over there. Then whoever is on the porch stands up and he's shouting something.

He steps into the porch light and throws a punch at a wooden post. "You need to learn to let shit go," he says.

Oh hell no.

I walk straight over there, rose in one hand and my car keys in the other. I shove the keys in my pocket and some tall skinny douchebag says, "Who the fuck is that?"

Bayleigh turns around, her eyes wide.

The guy, who I'm guessing is the idiot who got her grounded, walks to the end of the porch and glares daggers at me. Too bad he's not the least bit intimidating. "Bro, this has nothing to do with you," he says, holding out a hand as if his scrawny hand will actually stop me.

I step up on the porch, putting myself between her and this idiot. "It is my business if you're yelling at Bayleigh."

"Like hell it is," he says in this way that's trying to be all badass.

I ignore him and turn to Bayleigh. "For you," I say, handing her the rose. Even in the dim lighting I can see she's both terrified and blushing at the same time. I wink at her.

The douchebag shifts on his feet. "What the fuck is this? You're gone two weeks and you replace me with this dipshit?"

"I'm guessing you're Ian," I say.

He glares at Bayleigh and then looks at me. "If you know who I am then you know you need to leave now."

I shove my hands in my pockets and lean against the wall. "If you'd like directions back to the interstate, I'd be happy to help you out."

"I'm not going anywhere."

I lift an eyebrow. "I'm afraid you are."

Ian scowls then grabs Bayleigh's arm and tries pulling her to the other side of the porch. "Tell him I'm not going anywhere."

I let him do it, because it only fuels my anger right now. Bayleigh pulls out of his grip, her gaze going to the flower in her hand. "I'm sorry," she tells him, but she doesn't sound very sorry. "I think you need to go."

Ian is now so pissed he looks like he's going to burst into flames. I can't help the grin that spreads across my lips. There's no better way to win over a girl than by having her choose you. I'm not going to fight this idiot. I'm just going to stand here, leaning against the house, and wait for him to realize I'm the better man.

"Fuck both of you," Ian says as he steps off the porch and heads toward his car. "Don't bother calling me when you get home, Bayleigh." She doesn't say anything. He spits on the ground. "It's my fault for dealing with some whore still in high school."

Yeah, okay. That's where I draw the line.

I jump off the porch and grab his shoulder, turning him around so he can see what's coming to him. His eyes widen in horror. I'm just about to knock his fucking lights out when Bayleigh yells my name and grabs my arm.

I look at her and she's panting, her eyes wide, her hand holding my arm back. "Please don't," she whispers. Her eyes plead with me, and at first I think she's trying to save this bastard. But then I realize she's trying to save me. I don't need another assault charge and this guy looks like the kind of scum who would call the cops on me.

"Come on, Bayleigh," I say, linking my fingers into hers. "He isn't worth it."

While Ian curses and gets into his car, I take her inside. I walk her up the stairs and into her room, where she collapses on her bed, burying her head in her pillow. I sit next to her.

"I had no idea he was going to show up like that," she says after her tears have stopped.

I run a hand over her hair. "I figured as much when I heard him yelling at you."

She turns over, shifting onto her back. I lie down next to her and reach for her hand, pulling it to my chest.

"You shouldn't do that," she says.

"Why?" I ask. I turn sideways to look at her.

"Because you're leaving. Because holding my hand is a pointless comfort right now. It means nothing."

"It doesn't mean nothing to me."

She pulls her hand away. "You can't hold my hand, Jace. You can't kiss me and you can't bring me flowers. Because pretty soon you're leaving forever and I'll never see you again and it'll be the most pointless summer of my life."

I can't help it. I start laughing. She punches me in the arm and then I sit up and pull her into a sitting position next to me. "Bayleigh, Bayleigh, Bayleigh," I say, taking her face in my hands. "I have something exciting to tell you."

"Exciting for you, maybe." She pouts and looks away.

"Exciting for both of us," I say, trailing my hands down her arms until her fingers link into mine. "I just got back from Mixon Motocross Park."

"Okay…." She says, sounding less than excited.

"The owner offered me a job. My own motocross school—giving lessons and stuff at his track. It pays a lot of money and it's the perfect alternative since I can't race professionally anymore."

She bites her lip. "Where did you say this track is located?"

I smile because the GPS has already told me all I need to know. "About thirty minutes from your hometown."

Her eyebrows narrow. "What are you saying?"

I lean forward and place a soft kiss on her forehead. "I'm staying in Texas. I'm going to move to Mixon and work there. I'm not going back to LA."

"Are you sure?" Her voice is a whisper, her eyes soft.

I nod. "I have nothing in LA worth going back for. Here, I have you."

Her hesitant expression turns into a grin. I squeeze her hands and say, "That is, of course, if you'll be my girlfriend."

CHAPTER 15

Her smile is contagious. I've never been so happy in my life, and then she frowns and says, "Are you serious?"

Talk about taking the wind out of my sails.

"Yes," I say, still holding onto her hands because I'm afraid she'll slip away.

"Wow," she breathes. She looks down at her lap, at our intertwined hands. "I mean…wow. I didn't think you felt that way about me."

"How could you think that?" I bring her hand up to my lips and kiss her knuckles. "I've been pretty obvious about how I feel about you."

She shrugs. "Yeah, but then you said you were going back home."

"And I shouldn't have said that. Because I'm not. I can't leave you, not after I've totally fallen for you."

She blushes and that cute grin comes back. "Okay," she says, looking up at me through her eyelashes.

"Are you saying yes?" I ask.

She nods. "I'll be your girlfriend."

Warmth spreads through my entire body. I hadn't realized how much I needed her to say those words until she did just now. Now I am complete. Now I am happy. Nothing else matters other than her and me and this very moment.

I take her face in my hands and bring her lips to mine. She smells like green apple shampoo, and she sighs a little as I kiss her, and it's so adorable. I am so crazy about this girl.

Her hands slide up and around my neck and she holds me close. We're on her bed, but I don't try to take it any further. There will be plenty of time for that later.

For now, I want to take things slow, and get to know every single thing there is to know about my new girlfriend.

The End

Continue reading for bonus content!

I may be responsible for the first book, *Summer Unplugged*, but the rest of the series is all because of you, the readers. I remember very clearly when I wrote Summer Unplugged. I had an idea about a girl getting in trouble with her cell phone and having to go all summer without it. Even as an adult, I don't think I would survive that challenge. I started writing about the girl, and then when she got bored at her grandparent's house, I imagined the boy next door. I didn't want him to be just *any* boy, I wanted him to be the boy who would pull her out of the life she'd fallen into, a life of doing whatever it took to please some jerk who didn't even like her that much. I wanted Jace to be the kind of guy we all deserve. And so I wrote him that way.

This was originally just a sweet quick story I wrote for fun. I didn't even know if people would like it since it was a novella instead of a full length novel. But the next thing I knew, readers were asking me for more. I ended up writing a second book, and then a third. Then, because I was still getting requests for more of Jace and Bayleigh, I ended up writing an entire 10 book series! Then Becca's story was told and now recently I've published Jett's story. I am so grateful for my readers who have loved my characters so much that they asked me to grow this series into such a big thing!

I'm actually still getting requests for more of these characters and my answer is always: let's see what happens! I can't force out books if my heart isn't in them because then they'd be awful and it wouldn't do the characters' justice. So I have to wait until the characters inspire me to write a new part of their story. This is exactly how I wrote Unplugged Summer—a few weeks ago, I had the idea to see what Jace was thinking when this whole romance started. I hope you all enjoyed his story as much as I did!

FUN FACTS ABOUT SUMMER UNPLUGGED

- The first four books of the series are also available in audiobook. They are narrated by Cheryl Texiera, who is an actress that plays Maya's mom on the Disney Channel show, Girl Meets World. I was SO excited to work with her because I love that show and she did such an awesome job narrating the books!

- Mixon, Texas is a ghost town. When I work on a book, I like to set it in a town that's not currently real that way I don't have to worry about getting all the details right and I can make the town look how I want it to. However, instead of making up names, I search for Texas ghost towns and pick one from the list. Ghost towns are places that used to be a real town a hundred or more years ago, but over time people moved on to bigger cities and those towns faded into nothing. Most of them are just empty fields out in the middle of nowhere. Mixon is one of them. I liked the way Mixon sounds, so I adopted it for my own and made it into a bustling country town with a famous motocross track.

- Salt Gap is also a Texas ghost town!
- Summer Unplugged took 14 days to write. I started it in February of 2012.
- Unplugged Summer took 5 days to write. It was a little easier because I had the original document open next to the new one, and I copied all the dialogue over and then added Jace's perspective on each scene. I really enjoyed writing about his life before he met Bayleigh.
- I designed all of the book covers myself! I really like the cover art models even though they don't fully look like how I picture the characters in my head.

- The car Jace bought for Bayleigh was the exact car I owned at the time. Only I had to buy it myself. ;-)
- Lawson, Texas is another made up town in the series. You can find it in several other books I've written as well.
- Jace and Bayleigh's honeymoon was planned out entirely using Google maps and Google Earth. I've sadly never been to California, so I "traveled" virtually and found cool places for them to go.
- I was very nervous to write a book from Jace's point of view. I actually promised it to my readers and then when I sat down to plan the book, I got so scared that I wouldn't be able to do him justice! It was so challenging, but after a while, Jace's voice came to me and now I love writing from his perspective.

FREQUENTLY ASKED QUESTIONS ABOUT THE SUMMER UNPLUGGED SERIES

How did you come up with Jace and Bayleigh's names?

I chose Jace's name because I've always thought Jace was a cute name for a guy. (Shallow of me? Maybe!) One day I got my neighbor's mail on accident. I knew her daughter's name was "Bailey" but on the envelope, it was spelled Bayleigh, and I thought that was such a cool way to spell the name that it inspired me to use it for a character in my book. And thus, Bayleigh and Jace were created!

Why did you write about motocross?

I grew up in Texas and spent most of my childhood and teenage years on the dirt bike track.

Unlike Jace, I wasn't that great at racing or riding, but it was very fun! I met a ton of friends on the track and I'm still friends with them to this day. Motocross is such a fun sport and since motocross guys are totally hot, I knew I had to make Jace into one. :)

Will Summer Unplugged get made into a movie?

Unfortunately, as an author, I have absolutely no say so over this. I would totally love to see my story on the big screen, but usually the way that works is that a movie producer will seek out books they want to turn into movies. Another way is for a screen writer to turn the book into a script and then pitch it to movie producers. I currently have a screen writer friend who has talked about doing this in the future, but nothing is certain yet.

What is your favorite book in the series?

I want to say ALL OF THEM! But if I had to choose, I'd pick The Beginning of Forever because it's the wedding book. One thing I really love about Jace and Bayleigh is that their love of being together is more important than following clichés and trends. They had a small wedding and they did it their way and I really love that. They could have easily had some fancy thing that was very expensive, but they chose to celebrate their love their own way. I really love that!

Jace is so swoony. Is he based on someone you know in real life?

I wish! I get asked this a lot, but Jace is totally a figment of my imagination. As a romantic at heart, I often daydream sweet things for my stories because I love my characters and want them to have the best. Bayleigh deserves the best, don't you think? I wish I could say Jace is modeled after someone specific, but really he's just his own person, made up of what I think every boyfriend should have: loyalty, charm, love, respect, compassion.

My boyfriend acts like Ian. Should I dump him?

YES. Never date anyone who doesn't treat you with 100% respect at all times. You deserve respect and love.

Who is your favorite character from the series?

Bayleigh, because she's the voice of the story. I

saw most of the entire thing through her eyes and she reminds me a lot of how I was as a teenager; insecure, just wanting to please people. I think she turned into a really great friend, wife, and mother by the end of the series.

THE SUMMER UNPLUGGED SERIES

Part 1 - Summer Unplugged

Part 2 - Autumn Unlocked

Part 3 - Winter Untold

Part 4 - Spring Unleashed

Part 5 - The Beginning of Forever

Part 6 - Autumn Adventure

Part 7 - Winter Wonderful

Part 8 - The Girl with my Heart

Part 9 - Autumn Awakening

Part 10 - Winter Whirlwind

Part 11 - Unplugged Summer

Don't miss all of the spin-off series:

The Summer Series

The Believe in Love Series

The Team Loco Series

The Love on the Track Series

The Love at the Gym Series

The Summer Unplugged Epilogues

ABOUT THE AUTHOR

Amy Sparling is the *USA Today* bestselling author of books for teens and the teens at heart. She lives on the coast of Texas with her family, her spoiled rotten pets, and a huge pile of books. She graduated with a degree in English and has worked at a bookstore, coffee shop, and a fashion boutique. Her fashion skills aren't the best, but luckily she turned her love of coffee and books into a writing career that means she can work in her pajamas. Her favorite things are coffee, book boyfriends, and Netflix binges.

She started writing her own books in 2010 and now publishes several books a year. She also writes young adult and middle grade novels under the name Cheyanne Young.

Connect with her on at AmySparling.com